异语同心
THE WORDS WE SHARE

JACK WONG

annick
press
toronto · berkeley

安儿!
Angie!

"Package for Mr. Tang?"

"Yep, that's us!"

A lot of the time, when someone's at the door, Dad needs my help to speak to them.

Just like when we go out to eat, and Dad asks me to choose his meal from the menu. (Which means I also get to pick dessert!)

Or when we're at the store, and I have to double-check the labels to make sure he doesn't buy pet shampoo by mistake, like that one time.

Dad still speaks only in Cantonese.
We both knew just a tiny bit of English
when we first moved to Canada,
but I've learned lots at school since.
That's why I help him out sometimes.

A lot of things are harder for Dad here in our new country. He had trouble finding work too, until he found a job as a janitor. He didn't need to read or write for that—at first.

Then one evening after supper,
Dad lays out paper and markers
on the kitchen table.
Art time!

Not quite, he says—he's been given a new task at work, making some special notices around his building. He wants to tell me in Cantonese what the signs are supposed to say and have me write them out in English for him.

"I thought we were going to draw pictures," I want to say, but I can see Dad needs help.

At least Dad tries to make it fun.

These are brilliant—you're a pro! Dad says, beaming at me.

"Hey, I bet there are plenty of other people who need things written in English for them. Like signs for their store," I tell Dad. "I could start a business!"

If they should be so lucky! he says.

First, I go to Ms. Fong, who owns the canteen in Little Chinatown where we go for lunch sometimes.

太好了！我一直想在外面立个牌子。码头那边很多高级咖啡店都有。

*That would be wonderful!
I've always wanted to put
a sandwich board outside,
like those fancy cafés down
at the waterfront,* she says.

We make a deal that I'll update her sign
with the weekly lunch items.

I try Mr. Chu at the laundromat next.

"Some instructions for my machines would be good!" Mr. Chu agrees.
He's tired of customers always asking him how to use them,
with their worn-out buttons and dials.

Mr. Chu doesn't speak Cantonese like Ms. Fong or Ms. Lim, so he has to
dictate the steps to me in his English, which is quick and jumpy. I try to
write everything down as fast as I can.

Soon, everyone is noticing my signs!

安儿！
Angie!

A few days later, there's a call
on the phone—for me.

Another one of your happy customers! Dad says.

It's Mr. Chu—but he's not happy at all.
He tells me someone followed my instructions for
the laundry machine, and now all their clothes were shrunken,
and they were mad at him, and he sounds pretty mad at me.

I can feel my face hot against the phone.
I want to hide.

But the problem is, he can't—
he's the reason I'm writing
things in English for people
in the first place, and the last
person who could fix it.

All of a sudden I turn from hot
to cold. I feel very alone.

Come on, he says, *let's go down to see the owner together.*

My tummy is doing flip-flops by the time we get to the laundromat.

"Maybe we should come back later—" I start to say, but Dad squeezes my hand, and we go in.

When Dad greets Mr. Chu, the most bizarre thing happens—the voice that comes out of Dad's mouth is a complete stranger's!

It's making new sounds—not Cantonese, like when he speaks with me.

Then Mr. Chu makes the same sounds back. And they start laughing! Howling!

Their voices set everything around me spinning and waving, like an amusement park ride . . .

Or no—it's like when Dad and I arrived at the airport in Canada for the first time, on our shaky legs,

and everybody was speaking so fast around us, a swirl
of people and their strange music, it was all so new.

That's what this feels like.
Except this time Dad
is part of the strange music!

Then I realize both of them are now smiling at me—and Dad looks like Dad again.

"Well!" Mr. Chu says. Dad's had an idea.

Mr. Chu hands me a new sheet of paper. In the musical sounds, he explains to Dad how the machines work,

and Dad carefully relays each step to me.

It turns out they're speaking in another language with each other. It's Dad, not me, who's switching back and forth this time!

With Dad's help, I'm sure we got it right.

"Come back next week," Mr. Chu grins as we're leaving.
"You can help me with my flyers!"

I watch Dad as we walk home.
He looks changed, but also not.
Because the two languages
Dad knew how to speak perfectly
were in him this whole time.

What? he asks when he catches my eye.

". . . What did you say to get Mr. Chu
to laugh?" I ask.

哦，没什么。我们聊了聊才发现我们是同一个地方长大的。我们刚才说的是客家话，家乡那边常用。对了，我还给他讲了一个笑话：一件会说话的毛衣！

Oh, nothing. We just realized we both grew up in the same area back home. We were talking in Hakka, which is what people speak there. Wait—and I told him a joke about a talking sweater!

He shrugs it off with a laugh, but his eyes are shining as he squeezes my hand again.

It's late, so we stop by the diner for supper.

I make sure Dad knows all about the daily specials.

For dad, mom, and big sis

A Note from the Author

In this story, Angie discovers that her dad speaks another "language." Although the Hakka that Angie hears her dad using with Mr. Chu would sound quite different from the Cantonese that she and her dad speak at home, Hakka and Cantonese are similar in other ways; for this reason they are sometimes called different varieties or dialects of a family of languages called Chinese. One of the similarities between Cantonese and Hakka is their shared roots: both are commonly found in Southern China and Southeast Asia, including in Hong Kong (where I was born and learned Cantonese as my mother tongue). Another similarity is that both Cantonese and Hakka speakers (as well as speakers of other Chinese varieties you may have heard of, like Mandarin) read and write using the same Chinese characters, which is the writing you see on some of the pages of this book.

The Chinese title that you see on the cover is pronounced "Yee Yu Tong Sum" in Cantonese. In a reversal of Angie's story, it was me asking my mom for help to come up with this translation! Because ideas don't always translate directly from one language to another, she chose a title that means something like "The Same Heart in Different Languages." And how fitting! Even though the title isn't exactly the same as the one in English, she certainly captures the heart of the story with it.

My sincere thanks to Nina Wong (mom) and Li-Cheng Gu for their work on the title, and to my dear friend Jenny Yujia Shi for providing translations for the interior.

© 2023 Jack Wong (text and illustrations)

Cover art by Jack Wong, designed by Jack Wong and Sam Tse
Interior designed by Marijke Friesen

Edited by Katie Hearn

Annick Press Ltd.

We acknowledge the support of the Canada Council for the Arts and the Ontario Arts Council, and the participation of the Government of Canada/la participation du gouvernement du Canada for our publishing activities.

Canada

ONTARIO ARTS COUNCIL
CONSEIL DES ARTS DE L'ONTARIO
an Ontario government agency
un organisme du gouvernement de l'Ontario

Library and Archives Canada Cataloguing in Publication
Title: The words we share / Jack Wong.
Names: Wong, Jack, 1985- author, illustrator.
Identifiers: Canadiana (print) 20230154964 | Canadiana (ebook) 20230154972 |
ISBN 9781773217970 (hardcover) | ISBN 9781773217994 (HTML) |
ISBN 9781773218007 (PDF)
Classification: LCC PS8645.O459 W67 2023 | DDC jC813/.6—dc23

Published in the U.S.A. by Annick Press (U.S.) Ltd.
Distributed in Canada by University of Toronto Press.
Distributed in the U.S.A. by Publishers Group West.

Printed in China

annickpress.com
jackwong.ca

Also available as an e-book. Please visit annickpress.com/ebooks for more details.